Hit or Miss

Adapted by Laurie McElroy

Based on the series created by Michael Poryes and Rich Correll & Barry O'Brien

Part One is based on the episode, "Me And Mr. Jonas And Mr. Jonas And Mr. Jonas,"
Written by Douglas Lieblein

Part Two is based on the episode, "Everybody Was Best Friend Fighting," Written by Sally Lapiduss

DISNEP PRESS

New York

All rights reserved. Published by Disney Press, an imprint of
Disney Book Group. No part of this book may be reproduced
or transmitted in any form or by any means, electronic or
mechanical, including photocopying, recording, or by any
information storage and retrieval system, without written
permission from the publisher. For information address
Disney Press, 114 Fifth Avenue,
New York, New York 10011-5690.

Printed in the United States of America

First Edition
1 3 5 7 9 10 8 6 4 2
J689-1817-1-09319

Library of Congress Control Number: 2009926908
ISBN 978-1-4231-1811-4

For more Disney Press fun, visit www.disneybooks.com
Visit DisneyChannel.com

PART ONE

PART ONE

Chapter One

Miley Stewart drummed her fingers against the wall and sighed loudly. She was dressed as Hannah Montana and sitting in the hallway of a recording studio. A red bulb above the studio door was lit. A sign on the door read: DO NOT ENTER WHEN RED LIGHT IS ON. Whoever was in the studio was eating into her recording time, and Miley was getting impatient. She stood up and paced the hall, frowning.

Miley's father, Robby Ray Stewart, wasn't nearly as worked up. He was doing a crossword puzzle to pass the time. "Five-letter word: sixth president of the United States," he said.

Instead of answering, Miley groaned.

"That would work if his name was John Quincy *Ugh*," her father joked.

Miley shook her head. "Dad, I need to record now! What is taking so long?" she demanded. "Hannah is in the zone."

Hannah Montana was Miley Stewart's alter ego. By day, Miley was just like any other high-school girl. By night, she was pop-music sensation Hannah Montana. Miley loved being Hannah onstage. Offstage, she wanted to hang with her friends, go to school, and shop at the mall. Miley wanted people to like her for who she was, not just because she was famous.

In order to have a normal life, she kept her Hannah Montana identity a secret. When she was Hannah, Miley covered her long, brown wavy hair with a blond wig and traded in her T-shirt and jeans for glamorous sequins and suede.

Mr. Stewart was Hannah's songwriter and manager. He wore a disguise, too—a mustache and a hat. He knew his daughter well enough to recognize the real reason for her impatience. It had nothing to do with being in the zone, and everything to do with shopping.

"So what time is that big shoe sale you're meeting Lilly at?" he asked.

"Three-thirty," Miley admitted. "And you know all the sixes go first!"

"No, honey, I'm proud to say I don't know that," Mr. Stewart said. "Now what you need to do is just relax. Whoever is in there is just running a little late. They'll be done any minute."

Miley didn't want to relax. She wanted to record her song and get to that shoe sale. "They'll be done sooner than a minute," she said, grabbing the door handle.

"Hey!" Mr. Stewart yelled, trying to stop her.

He was too late. Miley had opened the door and marched into the studio.

A sound technician sat behind a panel of recording equipment. Three guys sat in a soundproof booth behind a glass window, putting the finishing touches on a song.

"Okay, who do you think you are?" Miley yelled. "The—"

She stopped short when she recognized who was recording. "Sweet mama!" she exclaimed. "It's the Jonas Brothers!"

The Stewarts had moved from Tennessee

to a beach house in Malibu, California, a few years ago, but that didn't stop Miley from lapsing into a country twang when she was surprised. Miley might have been a teen superstar, but she was also a teenage girl—and a big fan.

Kevin, Joe, and Nick Jonas were staring at her through the glass, wondering why she had interrupted their recording session.

Miley quickly pulled herself together and tried to act as if she wasn't the one who had barged into the studio. "Daddy, I told you somebody was in here," she said over her shoulder. Then she flipped a switch on the soundboard so the guys could hear her. "I am so sorry, guys. He gets so impatient."

Mr. Stewart walked in, rolling his eyes. "Sorry, fellas, I've got a big shoe sale I need to get to," he said wryly.

Nick hit his brother Joe on the arm.

"Dudes, it's Hannah Montana," Nick said.

Suddenly, the three brothers scrambled toward the door, each trying to be the first to say hello to Hannah in person. Kevin had almost gotten there when Joe jumped on his back. Then Nick tried to get past both of them. He was just about to open the door when Joe pulled him back and pushed his way past.

When they were finally standing in front of her, Miley was smiling, happy to know that they were as starstruck as she was.

"We're such big fans," Kevin told her.

"We love your music," Joe added.

Nick smiled at her with a dazed look on his face. "You're pretty," he said.

Kevin slapped his brother on the head.

"Uh, pretty good with the singing and the dancing that you do," Nick continued, trying to play it cool. Then he looked at

Miley again and couldn't help himself. "Wow, you're pretty," he repeated.

"Nice save," Kevin said sarcastically. He turned to Hannah and reached to shake her hand. "I'm Kevin," he said.

Miley knew exactly who he was. She shook his hand, smiling. "The cute, romantic one," she said. Then she took Joe's hand in both of hers. "And you're Joe, the cute, funny one." Finally she turned to Nick. "And you're Nick, the cute, sensitive one."

Nick stared at her, a dazed smile on his face.

Mr. Stewart stepped in front of Miley. He didn't exactly like the way the guys were looking at his daughter.

"You're Robby Ray!" Joe said, his eyes wide. Mr. Stewart's reputation for turning out hit songs was legendary in the music business. "He writes all the songs," Joe told his brothers.

"I know! 'Nobody's Perfect' is genius," Kevin said, naming one of Hannah's top-ten hits.

"I like the cute, romantic one," Mr. Stewart joked.

"I love how it starts all soft, and then — *bam*!" Joe said. He started to sing the chorus.

Kevin and Nick joined in. They all exchanged a high five when they were finished singing.

"I was wrong. I like them all," Mr. Stewart said.

"Step aside, cowboy. I saw them first," Miley told him. She wanted to get to know the Jonas Brothers, and she couldn't do that if they were focused on her father. "So, is it true you guys got discovered at a barber shop?" she asked.

"Yeah, funny story," Joe said. But instead of telling it, he turned to Mr. Stewart. He seemed to have forgotten all about Hannah Montana. "I can't believe how many hits you've written," he said.

Miley wasn't happy that the three cutest boys in the world were ignoring her and fascinated by her father. She stepped in between them. "Yep, Robby Ray writes them and Hannah sings them," she said pointedly.

"Uh-huh," Joe said, not taking his eyes off Mr. Stewart. He stepped forward, leaving Miley on the outside of the group.

"Sure," Kevin added.

Now it was Mr. Stewart, not Miley, who left Nick tongue-tied. "You're like a legend, dude. Uh, sir," he stammered. "Sir dude."

"Yep. He's the best, and he's all mine,"

Miley said with a chuckle. She pushed her way into the middle of the circle, trying to get the boys to notice her.

"Yeah. Uh-huh," Kevin said, pushing her right back out. He put his arm around Mr. Stewart's shoulders and started to lead him across the room. Miley followed them, not wanting to be left out. "You know what would be a great idea?" Kevin said to Mr. Stewart. "If you wrote a song for us."

"Yeah!" Joe said.

"That'd be awesome," Nick added.

Miley forced out a fake laugh. "I hate to disappoint you boys, but he only writes songs—"

She was about to say that her father only wrote songs for Hannah Montana, but Mr. Stewart cut her off. "I'd love to," he told the Jonas Brothers.

Miley did a double take. "Songwriting

daddy, say what?" she demanded.

Mr. Stewart didn't hear her. The Jonas Brothers were so excited he had agreed to write them a song that they drowned out Miley with their cheers. She stood outside the circle, watching them celebrate.

Chapter Two

Miley pulled a brush through Lilly Truscott's long blond tresses. She had offered to braid her best friend's hair while they waited for Mr. Stewart to get home from a meeting with the Jonas Brothers. He had been gone a lot longer than Miley expected. She couldn't stop thinking about her father having fun with another band. Miley focused all her frustration on her friend's hair. Lilly winced with each stroke of the brush.

Lilly was one of the few people who knew Miley was Hannah Montana. Lilly was also the one Miley had called when her father agreed to write for the Jonas Brothers.

"Where is Dad?" Miley demanded, forcefully weaving strands of Lilly's hair. "He was supposed to be home hours ago."

"*Ow!*" Lilly screamed.

Miley didn't notice. She was too busy ranting. "Stupid, cute Jonas Brothers!" she snapped.

"*Ow!*" Lilly said again. "You're braiding hair, not starting a chainsaw."

"I'm sorry. But they're guys, and he's a guy. What if he figures out that he likes writing for guys more than he likes writing for Hannah Montana?" Miley asked.

"Well, then you'll be out of work, and I'll be bald!" Lilly said.

"Lilly, this isn't funny. You should've seen the way they glommed on to him," Miley said, wrapping an elastic band around the end of the braid. She stood up and walked around the room, imitating the Jonas Brothers worshipping her father. "You are awesome! Will you write a song for us?" Then Miley imitated her father. "*Eeee*, doggies, I'd love to!" She flopped onto the couch and shook her head. "He was putty in their hands. Putty, I tell you!"

"Relax," Lilly said. "I'm sure your dad's just late because the Jonas Brothers are arguing about his music, or changing his lyrics, and making him miserable."

At that moment, Mr. Stewart walked through the front door, carrying his guitar case. "*Whoo*! I love the Jonas Brothers!" he said happily.

"Wow. I was way off," Lilly said.

Miley jumped to her feet and confronted her father. "Where have you been? You were supposed to be home two hours ago. Start talking, mister!"

"I'm sorry, honey, but time just got away from us," Mr. Stewart said, putting his guitar down. "One minute we're spitballing song ideas, the next thing I know we're having a spitball fight. Then we started playing air hockey and video games," he said, his voice rising with excitement. "It was a regular p-a-r-t-y. Party!"

Miley listened, her hands on her hips. Her father was supposed to be doing a job, not playing games. "You said you were working," she snapped.

"Well, it turns out I was. Listen to this." Mr. Stewart sang the first few lines of his new song, "We Got the Party."

Miley crossed her arms over her chest and rolled her eyes. She hated to admit it, but the song was good. So why did the Jonas Brothers get to sing it instead of Hannah Montana? she thought.

"Well, it's a lot cooler when the Jo-Bros do it," Mr. Stewart said. He headed to the kitchen and picked up the mail that was on the counter.

Miley turned to Lilly. "The Jo-Bros? He's even got a pet name for them," she said sadly.

"Oh, come on," Lilly said. "I'm sure he has a pet name for you, too."

"Yeah. Miley," she said sarcastically.

Mr. Stewart put down the mail. "I know it's not the way that I usually work, but goofing around with those boys is pulling a great song out of me. And look at this—"

Mr. Stewart faced away from the girls,

then turned around. He had circled one arm over his head and hooked the corner of his mouth with a finger, stretching his lips sideways. "Fish on a hook," he joked. "Joe taught it to me. You're right, he is the funny one."

"Yeah, hilarious," Miley said, teeth clenched.

Mr. Stewart didn't notice. "I've got to get on the webcam and show Uncle Earl!" he said, heading for the stairs. "He's going to love this."

Miley watched him go. "Okay, I don't care how cute they are. I hate those back-stabbing, Daddy-nabbing Jonas Brothers." She turned to Lilly for support, only to find her best friend trying out the fish-on-a-hook joke.

Lilly chuckled. "Hey, this is funny."

Miley shot her a furious look.

"If you're a stupid boy," Lilly said quickly.

At the beach that same afternoon, Miley's brother, Jackson, was warming up his muscles. He stretched to touch his toes, and then reached toward the sky.

He was standing in front of Rico's Surf Shop, a beach hangout where Jackson also worked. The shop was named after the owner's son. Rico was always ready to torment his older and taller employee. Today, he settled for an insult.

"Stretch all you want," Rico mocked. "You're not getting any taller. Trust me, I've tried."

"I may not be getting any taller, but I'm about to be a whole lot richer," Jackson said, doing a couple of side stretches.

"'How? You going to open a take-your-picture-with-an-idiot booth?'" Rico said, laughing at his own joke.

"'You going to open a take-your-picture-with-an-idiot booth?'" Jackson imitated in a whiny voice. Then he stood up as tall as he could. "No. Nakamora Sporting Goods is offering five thousand dollars to anyone who breaks the world record on the new Nakamora Extreme." He poured baby powder on his hands and rubbed them together. Then he shook powder down his shirt, wiggling so it went all over. Powder flew into the air like tiny snowflakes.

"Five big ones for riding a bike?" Rico asked.

"A bike? Please," Jackson said, scoffing. "The Nakamora Extreme is a precision instrument that requires a special blend of endurance, skill, and natural-born talent."

Rico rolled his eyes. If it required skill

and talent, he didn't believe Jackson could break any kind of record.

Jackson slipped a backpack on over his shoulders, and then put on a helmet. A tiny camera was attached to the helmet with a flexible rod. The lens was focused on Jackson's face.

"Let's do this," he said. He picked up the Nakamora Extreme—it was a pogo stick.

"In twenty hours and forty-two minutes, I'm going to be bouncing all the way to the bank," Jackson said. "Now, if you will excuse me."

Rico shook his head and walked off, convinced that Jackson would fail.

Jackson flicked a switch on his helmet. "Helmet-cam is a go. This is Jackson Rod Stewart, recording my hop to destiny," he said into the camera.

Jackson started to hop on the pogo stick.

He made it a few feet, then he landed on a hot dog and went flying. He hit the sand with a *thud*! He got to his feet, chuckling nervously, and started hopping again.

"Starting now. Once again, this is Jackson Rod Stewart hopping my way to history," he said into the camera. "I'm gonna be rich. I'm gonna be rich," he chanted. He hopped away, determined to ride the pogo stick to victory.

Chapter Three

While Jackson was trying to hop his way to wealth, Mr. Stewart was in the living room working on his song for the Jonas Brothers. He sang a verse and then leaned back. "Oh, those boys are going to love this," he said aloud to himself.

Miley crept quietly down the stairs. She had put on an old football jersey and a baseball cap. Her father had been obsessed with his new song since he got back from hanging with the Jonas Brothers. Miley had a plan to make sure he paid attention to her—and only her—all afternoon. If playing silly boy games inspired him to write hit songs, then she would play, too.

Miley blew through a straw, sending a spitball into the back of her father's head.

"Hey, what the—" Mr. Stewart put his hand to his head. He turned around and spotted Miley and her straw. "What are you doing?"

"I'm just goofing off, getting those creative juices flowing," Miley told him. "Try it with me, Daddy. You know, spit-balling could pull a great song out of you." She blew another spitball at him.

"Are you okay?" Mr. Stewart asked curiously. Since when did Miley shoot spitballs? he wondered.

"Never better! Just hanging out with

my old man!" Miley punched him on the arm and grunted as if she were a boy. "Hey, Daddy, why don't we have an arm-tooting contest? I'll go first." She put her fist under her arm and made loud armpit farts. "Beat that!" she challenged.

"Honey, I don't have time for this," Mr. Stewart said. "I'm trying to finish this song."

Miley didn't understand. He had time to play with the Jonas Brothers, but not with her? Were they more important to him than she was? "But, Dad—"

Mr. Stewart's cell phone rang.

"Excuse me," he said, cutting off Miley. "Hello? No, there's no one here by the name of Gunner," he said into the phone. "Sorry, this isn't the Tinkle residence."

Why didn't he hang up and talk to her? Miley wondered, frustrated. It was obviously a wrong number.

"Well, I don't care what you say," Mr. Stewart said into the phone. "I'm not Gunnar Tinkle." Suddenly he understood. It was a prank call, and he had a good idea who had made it. "Gonna tinkle! Joe, is that you?"

Across town, all three Jonas Brothers were on a speakerphone. They cracked up laughing.

"We so own you," Joe said.

"Busted!" Nick yelled.

"That was sick!" Kevin added.

"Oh, you boys. LOL," Mr. Stewart said.

Miley couldn't believe it. Her father knew the slang for laugh out loud? Since when? "You know LOL?" she asked.

Mr. Stewart covered the mouthpiece of his phone. "Yeah, Nick taught it to me." Then he spoke into the phone again. "Hey, you guys want to hear the chorus of your new song?" he asked.

"Yeah!" Kevin and Joe said.

"Go for it!" said Nick.

"It's a little rough," Mr. Stewart told them. He put the phone down and made a couple of loud armpit farts.

The Jonas Brothers laughed again.

"Beat that!" Mr. Stewart said. "Oh, sorry. Hold on. I'm getting another call." He pushed a button on his phone. "Hello? What? Amanda? Amanda Hugginkiss?" He realized he was being pranked again. "A man to hug and kiss? Miley, I don't have time for this foolishness. I'm trying to work here."

Across the room, Miley was crouched behind the kitchen table, talking into her cell phone. "So am I!" she said, standing up. "I'm inspiring you with my humor!

Dad, listen to this one. So why was six afraid of seven?" She waited for a moment, then answered her own question. "Because seven ate nine!" She laughed loudly. "*Whoo!* That is hysterical. Hang up and we could write a hit."

Mr. Stewart rolled his eyes and switched back to his other call. "Sorry, guys. It was just my daughter being silly."

Miley made a face and closed her cell phone. When the Jonas Brothers threw spitballs and pranked him, he called it inspiration. When Miley did the same thing, he called her silly. What was going on? Was she losing her father to the Jonas Brothers?

Mr. Stewart didn't notice Miley's sad expression. He was talking on his phone. "Yeah, well sure. Of course. I'll be right over." He hung up and jumped to his feet, rubbing his hands together as if he couldn't wait to get where he was going. "Hey, darlin', I'm going to go meet the boys and finish this song," he said.

"But, Daddy, what about we just hang out today?" Miley said.

At that moment, Lilly rolled into the room on her skateboard.

"Hey, here's Lilly to keep you company," Mr. Stewart said, grabbing his guitar and putting on his hat. "You guys have a good night, now." He walked out with a bounce in his step.

Lilly watched him go. "He looks happy."

"Of course he's happy. He's hanging out with . . ." Miley made a face to show her disgust. ". . . them," she said.

"Oh, my gosh! Your dad's having a bromance," Lilly exclaimed.

"Worse! He's having a Jo-Bro-mance,"

Miley said. "I used to be the one that he loved to write for. Now, they're all he thinks about. Why aren't I enough anymore? Give me one good reason!"

"Well, they're new, there's three of them, and they're *soooo* cute," Lilly said.

That was not what Miley wanted to hear. She needed sympathy, not more reasons why her father had thrown her over for the Jonas Brothers. "I said one," she snapped.

"Right." Lilly cleared her throat and tried to share Miley's anger. "And to think, you gave him the best fourteen years of your life. Years you will never get back."

"Exactly!" Miley agreed. "I am not about to get thrown away like yesterday's moo-shu pork!" she yelled angrily, putting her hands on her hips.

"You had moo-shu pork yesterday? Is

there any left?" Lilly asked eagerly. She ran toward the kitchen.

"Lilly! Focus!" Miley yelled, stopping her. "I am not about to let Larry, Curly, and Moe-Bro waltz in and steal him away!"

Lilly looked confused, not understanding Miley's comparison of the Jonas Brothers and the Three Stooges.

Miley raised her arm and pointed her index finger toward the ceiling. "My daddy writes for me and nobody else," she said.

"So what are you going to do?" Lilly asked.

Miley might have been jealous. She might have been outraged. She might have felt completely overlooked by her father. But she had to admit that she didn't have an answer to Lilly's question. "I have no idea," she admitted.

While Miley was coming up with a plan, Jackson was still trying to hop his way to five thousand dollars.

"Pardon me! Breaking a record!" he yelled as he bounced around a group of surfers on the beach. This is hard work, he thought. Suddenly, his stomach growled. "Getting hungry!" he shouted.

At Rico's Surf Shop, Lilly was eating lunch at one of the tables. She threw a hot dog in Jackson's direction, and he caught it in his mouth.

"Thank you," he mumbled, hopping away.

Lilly was watching him go when Miley ran up.

"Lilly! I figured out how to get my daddy back!" she said.

"How?" Lilly asked.

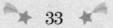

Miley sat across from her best friend and grinned. She had a brilliant plan. "Okay, the Jo-Bros aren't going to want to record Dad's song if they know he stole it from another guy band."

"What guy band?" Lilly asked, confused. She knew Mr. Stewart would never steal a song from anyone.

Miley said nothing. She simply smiled and nodded.

Lilly's eyes widened. She knew where this crazy plan was going, and it wasn't a place she wanted to visit. "Oh, no."

Miley pulled a piece of hair under her nose, and held it there like a mustache. "Oh, yeah," she said.

A couple of hours later, the girls headed to the recording studio. They had disguised themselves as two guys who looked as if they were in a heavy-metal rock 'n' roll band.

Miley's long brown hair was covered in a short, spiky blond wig. She had glued a patch of hair to her chin. Jeans, a flannel shirt, and a black leather vest completed her disguise.

Lilly wore a similar outfit, except her wig was dark brown, and she had used an eyeliner pencil to draw what looked like stubble on her chin.

Both girls wore leather wrist cuffs with metal studs, heavy chains around their necks, and sunglasses.

"I can't believe I'm going to meet the Jonas Brothers," Lilly said in an excited, high-pitched squeal.

"Guy voice," Miley reminded her in a deep voice.

"I can't believe I'm going to meet the

Jonas Brothers," Lilly said again, except this time her voice was deeper and she was trying to look tough.

Both girls took off their sunglasses and nodded. "Yeah," they said together, in the most masculine voices they could muster.

Would they be able to fool three real guys—the Jonas Brothers? Miley wondered.

Chapter Four

At Rico's Surf Shop, Jackson was doing his best to win the pogo-stick contest. He hopped up to the snack bar. "Rico, I've got to use the bathroom."

"That ought to be interesting," Rico said.

"Just open the door!" Jackson pleaded desperately.

A few hours ago, Rico wouldn't have thought Jackson could actually break the record. But now . . . "Sure," he said. "For half your winnings."

"Dude, I am not going to split five thousand doll—"

"*Whoops.*" Rico cut Jackson short as he poured a glass of water on the snack bar. "Look at that," Rico said. "Drip, drip, drip."

Jackson looked at the water. Now he really had to go to the bathroom. He had no choice. Either he gave Rico half of his winnings, or he was going to have an extremely embarrassing accident. He crumbled. "Okay, deal! Partner," he said. "Open the door."

Rico opened the door, and Jackson hopped inside the bathroom.

A few moments later, the toilet flushed. Rico opened the door again, and Jackson hopped out, still on the pogo stick.

"Mission accomplished," Jackson said. Then he gave a rundown for the camera. "He shoots, he scores! Nothing but bowl!"

Now that Rico was a partner, he really cared about Jackson's performance. Later that afternoon, Jackson's energy started to fail. Rico was there with a big bucket of water, and he was only too happy to throw it in Jackson's face!

Miley knew exactly what time the Jonas Brothers were supposed to get to the recording studio, and she and Lilly were ready for them.

When the brothers arrived, they were in the middle of a marshmallow fight. They ran through the halls and launched candy at each other.

"Eat marshmallow, fro-bro!" Joe said, hitting Nick in the head with candy.

"Chew on this, sucker!" Nick shouted as he fired back.

Kevin ran into the hall and launched marshmallows at both of his brothers. "Put this in your cocoa!"

"Hey, let's blast Robby Ray," Joe suggested.

"Great idea," Nick said.

"But it's three against one," Kevin said. He adjusted his protective goggles and grinned. "I like it!"

Shouting, they burst through the door of the studio and filled the sound technician's booth with flying marshmallows.

Instead of Mr. Stewart, two guys in leather motorcycle vests were there.

Wearing their disguises, Miley and Lilly turned around. They pretended to be annoyed at the interruption.

"Yo, we're working here," Miley said in

a gruff, low voice. She pumped her fist in the air.

Even though Lilly had mastered a guy's voice, she wasn't quite sure what guys said to each other. "Yeah, dudes. Be cool, dudes. Yo." She gave her armpit a scratch for good measure. Then she sniffed her hand. Gross! she thought, making a face.

"Uh, sorry, guys," Kevin said. "We got a text from the guy we're working with. He told us to be here early. Our bad."

Miley knew all about that text. She was the one who had sent it from her father's cell phone. She and Lilly would be gone before Mr. Stewart showed up. With any luck, the Jonas Brothers would be gone, too. At least from her father's life, Miley hoped.

"No big," she said in a low voice. She waved her arms around while she talked, trying to imitate some of the boys at her school. "We're just working on our guy-band stuff. So, if *you* guys want to hang until *we* guys are done, that's cool. Because we're all, you know . . ." Miley pounded her fist on her chest twice. ". . . guys."

Lilly mirrored Miley's bizarre body language and nodded.

The Jonas Brothers looked at each other with confused expressions. These two guys seemed very weird.

"Okay, sure," Joe said slowly.

Nick decided to introduce himself and his brothers. "This is Joe and Kevin, and I'm Nick," he said.

"We know who you are," Miley said. "Your music rocks!"

"And you're so hot," Lilly added. Then she realized how strange that sounded in her guy voice. Plus it was definitely not something most guys would say.

The Jonas Brothers looked at each other again, even more confused.

Miley jumped in to save the conversation. "On the charts! Burning them up! Yeah!" She pumped her fist again and tried to look tough.

"Yeah, that's what I meant . . . dudes," Lilly said. Then she threw in another "yo."

"So, who are you guys?" Kevin asked.

Miley stuck out her hand. "I'm Mi—" Then she paused. Quickly she pulled back her hand before anyone could shake it. "—lo," she finished. "Milo."

"And I'm Otis," Lilly said.

"Right," Miley said, "we're Milo and Otis." Realizing what she had just said, she glared at Lilly.

Lilly shrugged. It was the best she'd been able to come up with on the spot.

"So, what are you guys working on?" Joe asked.

"New song we just wrote," Miley said.

"Ourselves," Lilly added. "We wrote it. Milo and Otis. Two guys." She noticed that the Jonas Brothers were staring. Did they suspect she was a girl? "Football!" she shouted. She flexed her arms as if she were a bodybuilder.

"They get it," Miley said. "Let's play it for them."

"Coolio!" Lilly shouted. Just in case the Jonas Brothers still suspected her, she yelled out the most guylike thing she could think of: "Monster trucks!"

The girls headed into the recording booth. Miley picked up an electric guitar, and Lilly grabbed a mike. They launched into an incredibly bad, incredibly loud, heavy-metal version of Mr. Stewart's new song. No one would call what they were doing singing, but somewhere in the middle of their grunts and off-key shouts, the Jonas Brothers recognized the lyrics to the song Mr. Stewart had written for them.

"That's . . . that's our song. . . . Isn't it?" Joe asked.

"I can't hear you," Kevin said. "My ears are full of melted brain."

"I kind of liked it," Nick said.

As soon as the girls were finished screaming the song, the Jonas Brothers stormed into the recording booth.

"So, do we, like, rock or what?" Lilly asked.

"What'd you think?" Miley asked.

"I think that's our song," Kevin said, confronting them.

"What?" Miley and Lilly asked together.

"Robby Ray wrote that song for us," Joe said.

"Oh, man!" Miley said.

Lilly growled. "Robby Ray, that lying, cheating, stinking, stealing—"

"Easy, Otto," Miley said, cutting her off.

"Ot-*tis*," Lilly said, correcting her, but at the same time mispronouncing her own name. "Otis," she said quickly.

"Right," Miley agreed.

The Jonas Brothers were so focused on their stolen song that they didn't seem to notice that Milo and Otis weren't quite sure of their own names.

"What are you talking about?" Nick asked.

"Robby Ray didn't write that song," Miley said. "He stole it from us. He came in while we were rehearsing and said he was just *listening*." She made air quotes with her fingers.

Miley was a good actress. The Jonas Brothers seemed to believe her.

"Unbelievable," Kevin said, shaking his head with disgust.

"He ripped you off?" Nick asked.

Miley nodded. "Totally."

"Robby Ray hurt us," Lilly said. "He hurt us deep."

"Way deep, man. In the gut," Miley added. She tapped her fist against her stomach to prove her point.

"And then he lies to us. How bogus is that?" Kevin asked, outraged. Stealing another band's song and passing it off as original was beyond uncool.

Joe shook his head. "I feel so used."

"You?" Nick asked. "I shared my nachos with that guy!"

The brothers were reacting exactly the way Miley wanted them to.

"I don't even want to see this guy again. I'm out," Kevin said. He headed toward the door.

"Sorry, guys," Joe said to Miley and Lilly. "It's your song. Are we cool?"

Miley nodded. "We're cool." She held up her hand for a fist bump. Joe hit his fist against hers a lot harder than Miley had expected. She shook her hand to relieve the pain.

"No hard feelings?" Nick asked, holding out his hand to Lilly.

Lilly hated the fact that she was this close to her favorite guy band and couldn't even get a hug. She saw her chance and took it. "Nothing a hug wouldn't fix," she said in a gruff voice. She slapped Nick's hand aside and threw her arms around him.

Nick tried to pull away, but Lilly held on.

"Otis," Miley said. Her voice held a

warning, but her best friend ignored it.

Lilly kept hugging. A confused Nick patted her on the back.

"Otis!" Miley snapped.

Lilly jumped back, breaking the hug.

"That dude smells really good," Nick said to his brothers as they walked out.

Miley closed the door and grinned. "And that is what happens when you try to steal Miley Stewart's daddy!" she said. Her plan had gone perfectly. The Jonas Brothers would be gone before her father arrived. No one would ever know the part she had played to make sure that Mr. Stewart continued to write for Hannah Montana, and only Hannah Montana.

Just then, Lilly looked out the recording booth window and saw Mr. Stewart walk into the sound technician's room. "Funny you should mention him," Lilly said.

Miley looked out the window. She saw that the Jonas Brothers were still there, and they were glaring at her father.

"Oh, sweet niblets!" she yelled, yanking Lilly to the floor.

"What are we going to do?" Lilly asked.

"Okay," Miley said, "we still have a chance. Maybe they'll be so angry, they won't even talk to him."

"Right," Lilly whispered.

The girls peeked out the window, then hit the floor again. Mr. Stewart and the Jonas Brothers were definitely speaking.

"Okay, they're talking," Miley said. "But that doesn't necessarily mean that they're telling him about us."

"Okay. All right," Lilly said.

The girls looked over the windowsill again. They popped their heads up just as the Jonas Brothers turned around and pointed in their direction. Mr. Stewart was looking, too, and there was no question that he recognized Miley and Lilly.

Eek! Miley squeaked.

Mr. Stewart waved.

The only thing Miley and Lilly could do was wave back.

Miley knew she was in trouble—big trouble.

Chapter Five

At the beach, Jackson was in trouble, too. He was exhausted. If he didn't break the record soon, he would have to give up. "How . . . much . . . longer?" he said to Rico, panting.

Rico checked his watch. "Just a few more minutes, champ. You're almost there. Hop, kangaroo boy! Hop!"

A crowd had formed around them. "Hop! Hop! Hop!" the group chanted.

"Ah! Can't . . . hop. Must . . . stop,"
Jackson wheezed. He tried to keep going,
but his leg muscles buckled. He fell back
and hit the ground with a *thump*!

The crowd groaned and walked away.

"No!" Jackson said with a moan. "I was
hops away from history, and I couldn't
do it."

"Oh, you hopped into history four hours
ago," Rico told him.

"What?" Jackson asked.

"You broke the record four hours
ago," Rico said, grinning. "I just wanted to
see how long you could go."

"Because of you, I've been bouncing for
four hours with a wedgie I'll probably
need surgery to remove?" Jackson asked.
He couldn't believe it. That was four hours
of torture he hadn't needed to endure.

"Yep," Rico said proudly. "Aren't I a

stinker?" There was nothing that he loved more than messing with Jackson. Plus, he'd just won half the prize money. He started to walk away.

"C'mere," Jackson said, trying to grab Rico. He didn't have the energy to chase him.

"Uh-uh." Rico shook his head and stayed where he was. He knew Jackson was too exhausted to pursue him.

"I'm going to get you." Jackson tried to stand up and go after Rico, but his legs were too tired after all those hours of hopping. He fell back down.

"Doubt it," Rico said, laughing.

"Rico!" Jackson yelled, crawling after him. "No!"

Rico laughed. Then he skipped out of Jackson's reach but stayed just close enough to torment him.

✿ ✿ ✿

Miley and Lilly had escaped from the recording studio as fast as they could. They didn't want to see the Jonas Brothers again, and they definitely did not want to face a very angry Mr. Stewart. Lilly had gone home. Miley hid in her bedroom.

When Miley heard her father's car pull into the driveway, she headed for the balcony outside her room. From there, she climbed up onto the roof. It was a place she went when she was feeling sad. Today she was feeling more than sad. She was scared, too. Scared that she was going to lose her father to the Jonas Brothers.

Mr. Stewart knew exactly where to look for his daughter. He walked out onto the balcony and looked up at his daughter on the roof. "Hey, Mile. I guess you know we're going to have to talk about this sooner or later."

"Don't worry, Daddy. Hannah already called the Jonas Brothers and told them that she hired Milo and Otis, and it was all a prank," Miley said. "So you can run off and go play air hockey with your new best friends. I'm sure it's a lot more fun than hanging around with boring old me."

"Okay, see ya!" Mr. Stewart teased. He turned around and headed for the door.

"Daddy!" Miley yelled.

Mr. Stewart turned back. His face softened when he saw how sad and upset Miley was. "Honey, you can't seriously be jealous of me spending time with the Jonas Brothers."

"You're having so much fun writing for them," Miley said. She climbed down off the roof, but she couldn't look her father in the eye. She crossed her arms over her chest and gazed at the ocean. "That song you wrote is really good. They're just going to keep wanting more, Dad, and then other people will, and then . . ."

Miley stopped. She couldn't say the rest out loud. It was too painful.

Mr. Stewart knew what his daughter was thinking. "And then I won't have time for Hannah Montana?" he finished.

"Or Miley," she said sadly. She sat down on a bench.

"Now, darlin', let me tell you something," Mr. Stewart said, sitting down next to her. "You know, I could write a hundred songs for those boys. But there's one thing I can't do. And that's put my arm around them and say they're my little girl." Mr. Stewart put his arm around Miley and pulled her toward him. "Well, I could, but it'd be extremely weird," he said, teasing her.

Miley smiled. "So you're not bored with me?" she asked.

"Bored with you? I *love* writing songs for Hannah Montana," Mr. Stewart replied. "Almost as much as I love being Miley's daddy."

Miley leaned back and rested her head on her father's shoulder with a smile. Why had she been so jealous? she wondered. Her father loved her.

"You know, it's a shame you didn't like those boys, though, because I had this vision about getting them and Hannah together," Mr. Stewart said.

Miley sat up. Hannah Montana and the Jonas Brothers? Now that was something that could make her smile. "Hold on, Pops. I said I didn't like them spending so much time with you. Now, with me? That would be off the hook." Miley wrapped her arm around her head and grabbed the corner of her mouth with her index finger, copying her father's joke. "Get it? Off the hook."

A few days later, Miley and the Jonas Brothers were together again in the recording studio.

This time, Miley wasn't disguised as a heavy-metal rock 'n' roll dude. She was wearing her blond wig, and there was no black leather in sight. This time, she was Hannah Montana.

She sang the opening lines of Mr. Stewart's new song, "We Got the Party." Kevin and Nick both played guitar and sang. Joe took some of the vocals. They sang the chorus together. It was a rockin' song, and Miley hoped her fans liked it as much as she did.

That night, they decided to try out the song in front of a live audience. So Hannah Montana and the Jonas Brothers gave a surprise concert in front of Rico's Surf Shop. Jackson, Rico, all of Miley's friends, and most of her high school classmates were there.

Of course, no one except her closest friends and family knew that Hannah was really Miley.

Dressed in white jeans, a white T-shirt, a rockin' turquoise jacket, and, of course, her blond Hannah wig, Miley gave the performance her all. She even hopped up on a table partway through the song.

The Jonas Brothers played guitar and drums, and sang, too.

As Miley sang, she watched the crowd around her. Her friends, including Lilly and Oliver, were dancing to the music. The song seemed to be a hit, and it did exactly what the lyrics described—created a party in an instant.

Working with the Jonas Brothers had turned out to be a lot of fun. Miley had realized that she didn't need to be jealous. She knew that her father would never grow bored of Hannah Montana, or of her.

Miley had only one question left about the Jonas Brothers: which one of them was the cutest?

Miley was still pondering that question the next day when she and Mr. Stewart arrived at the recording studio.

Miley, disguised as Hannah Montana, was on a mission with her dad, who was dressed as Hannah's manager. They both carried marshmallow launchers and wore protective goggles.

Mr. Stewart looked around a corner and whistled to Miley. She ran forward, and she and her dad stood on either side of the door to the recording room.

"Ready, darlin'?" Mr. Stewart asked.

"Oh, yeah," Miley replied, nodding.

They tiptoed into the sound technician's booth, careful to stay away from the window so that the Jonas Brothers wouldn't see them.

"All right, Daddy, you take Joe and Kevin. Nick is all mine," Miley said. She burst through the door to the recording room, shooting marshmallows. "Eat this, suckers!" she shouted.

Mr. Stewart was right behind her.

There was just one problem. The marshmallows didn't hit the Jonas Brothers. A gospel choir was in the sound booth, and they were in the middle of recording,

"Dad, I need to record now! What is taking so
long? Hannah is in the zone," Miley said.

Why didn't her dad hang up and talk to her? Miley
wondered. It was obviously a wrong number.

"Oh, my gosh! Your dad's having a bromance," Lilly exclaimed.

Miley and Lilly introduced themselves to the Jonas Brothers as Milo and Otis.

The Jonas Brothers pointed to Miley and Lilly. There was no question that Mr. Stewart recognized them.

"I *love* writing songs for Hannah Montana," Mr. Stewart said. "Almost as much as I love being Miley's daddy."

Hannah Montana and the Jonas Brothers gave a surprise concert in front of Rico's Surf Shop.

Miley and Mr. Stewart prepared to burst into the recording studio carrying marshmallow launchers.

Part Two

"A vampire? Really?" Miley asked Oliver. "Was your wolf-man costume at the cleaners?"

"Hannah backstage rule number one: be calm. Be cool," Miley said.

"You can call me Gui," Guillermo said, taking
Lilly's hand and kissing it.

"I can't pay, but I'll gladly tell your fortune for
a water," Madame Escajeda told Rico.

"I'm going to be serving it up with the cutest guy in tennis!" Miley said.

Lilly and Oliver both wanted to go to the tennis tournament, and they were willing to fight for it.

"One little itty-bitty thing . . . Guillermo Montoya
never loses!" Guillermo said. "Never!"

"Hello!" Miley yelled. "Girl wrapped in a net here."

"When the Saints Go Marching In."

"*Whoopsies,*" Miley said.

"Wrong studio," Mr. Stewart explained, chuckling nervously.

"Our bad," Miley said. "Keep on marching in."

They left the room, closing the door behind them. What had happened to the Jonas Brothers? Miley wondered.

"Where are they?" she asked.

"I don't know," her father said. "They promised they were going to be here."

As Miley and Mr. Stewart stepped into the hallway, they realized they were in trouble.

Joe was pointing his marshmallow launcher at them. Nick and Kevin stood right behind him.

"And we always keep our promises!" Joe shouted.

"Duck and cover, Daddy!" Miley said.

"It's the return of the Jonai!"

It was too late. Miley and Mr. Stewart were pelted with marshmallows. But Miley didn't mind. The silly boy games she'd scoffed at had turned out to be a lot more fun than she'd expected. Plus, who knew — one of them might lead to another hit song!

PART TWO

Chapter One

"**M**iley!" Mr. Stewart yelled up the stairs. "Unless you want to do sound check in front of an audience, you best make like a cow and *moo*ve!"

Miley's dad was standing in the living room, impatiently waiting for Miley and Lilly. Hannah had a concert that night, and they were leaving later than they should be. Mr. Stewart grabbed his car keys and pulled on his jacket.

Miley and Lilly ran down the stairs. Miley was dressed as Hannah Montana for that night's concert. She was wearing a blond wig and a black-and-white outfit.

Lilly wore a disguise, too. When she hung out with Hannah Montana, Lilly called herself Lola Luftnagle and wore bright outfits and colorful wigs. Today's wig was purple.

Mr. Stewart picked up his guitar case. "What the heck takes you girls so long?" he asked.

"Wig," Miley answered.

"Makeup," Lilly said.

Miley struck a pose. "Wardrobe."

Both girls held out their wrists to show off their bracelets. "Bling!" they said together.

"And then you hate it and have to start all over again," Miley explained. Getting ready was more than just a simple matter of putting on clothes, makeup, and jewelry. It had to be the right clothes, makeup, and jewelry.

Just then, Miley's other best friend, Oliver Oken, walked in. Oliver, like Lilly, knew Miley's secret. "Oh, good. You guys are still here," he said.

"Yeah, and trying hard not to be," Mr. Stewart told him. "So whatever it is you're here for, make it quick. We don't have time for another bling crisis."

"Well, I was just coming to wish Miley luck at the concert," Oliver said. "Which I won't be going to . . ." He turned to Miley with a pointed expression. " . . . again."

"Oliver, you know if you want a ticket, all you have to do is ask me," Miley said.

"Oh, great. Can I have three?" Oliver asked. "One for me and my two best friends. Oh." He forced out a fake-sounding chuckle. "Wait a minute, they'll already be there. Backstage, where I wasn't invited—*again*."

Lilly rolled her eyes.

"Dang it, Oliver. This is my favorite outfit, and now you're getting guilt all over it," Miley said, teasing him.

"Oh, don't worry," Lilly said. "We'll open the windows in the limo and it will blow right off." She blew on the palm of her hand to demonstrate. Then she grabbed Miley's arm and pulled her toward the door. "Let's go."

"Oh, sure, make jokes," Oliver said sarcastically. "I'll go home and laugh at them alone . . . *again*."

Lilly was used to hearing this. She mouthed the word "alone" at the same time Oliver said it.

Miley had been teasing Oliver, but now she really was beginning to feel guilty. Oliver was right—she never invited him to her Hannah Montana events. "Well . . ."

Lilly could guess what Miley was thinking, and she didn't like the direction her mind was going in. "Miley! Conference," she said. She dragged her friend into the kitchen. "You're not actually thinking about this, are you?" Lilly asked.

"Well, he's never been backstage to anything," Miley said.

On the other side of the room, Oliver sighed loudly.

"I know this is kind of our special thing," Miley continued, "and you might be kind of jealous, but—"

"Jealous?" Lilly scoffed, cutting her off. "I am . . . I am not jealous."

Lilly's stammer gave her away. She

didn't want to share her Hannah Montana experiences with Oliver.

"Yes, you are," he shouted from across the room.

"I am not talking to you," Lilly said. She turned back to Miley. "Look, I just don't want you to be embarrassed, okay? Let's face it, he's just not as sophisticated as Lola Luftnagle, international jet-setter." She threw open her arms and yelled, "Bam!" to demonstrate. She accidentally knocked everything off the kitchen counter.

"Oh, and *I'm* embarrassing?" Oliver asked sarcastically.

"Fine, you're in," Miley told him.

Oliver turned to Lilly. "Ha!"

"What?" Lilly asked. She threw out her arms again, and this time she knocked over a pot. She tried to catch it as it clattered to the floor. "I meant to do that," she said.

❄ ❄ ❄

A few hours later, Miley was onstage performing as Hannah Montana. Her strong, clear voice filled the concert arena. She brought her hit song "Make Some Noise" to a close. The audience cheered enthusiastically. Miley ran backstage for a quick break. A stagehand gave her a bottle of water, then Miley ran over to Lilly.

"Hey, has Oliver gotten here yet?" Miley asked.

"No. He texted me he's having a little trouble putting together a disguise." Lilly chuckled and shook her head, trying to imagine what Oliver would come up with. "This ought to be good."

"Will you relax?" Miley said. "I'm sure everything is going to be fine."

She had just taken a sip of water when Oliver burst through the double doors that

led to the backstage area. He was wearing a vampire cape over a black suit. He had dyed his hair with what looked like black shoe polish, then combed it back away from his face. He had also used the shoe polish to give himself an incredibly fake-looking widow's peak, and he was wearing black lipstick.

"Good evening," Oliver announced with a fake Transylvanian accent. He spotted Miley and Lilly and made his way over to them, twirling his cape dramatically. "Let's pump some blood into this party!" he said.

Miley was so shocked that she spit out her water, spraying it all over Lilly.

"A vampire? Really?" Miley asked, teeth clenched. "Was your wolf-man costume at the cleaners?"

"Will you relax?" Lilly repeated. "I'm sure everything's going to be fine."

"Stop enjoying this!" Miley snapped.

"Hey, this is the best I could do on short notice," Oliver said. "If I was invited earlier, I would have had time to—"

"Grow some fangs?" Miley asked sarcastically.

"Oh, I forgot. Hold on," Oliver said. He faced away from Miley and Lilly, then slipped something into his mouth. When he turned around, he was wearing fangs.

Miley had to get back onstage, but she couldn't leave Oliver dressed like that. If people realized that Hannah Montana's friends were wearing disguises, which Oliver's costume made obvious, they might start digging for information. It wouldn't take long for a suspicious reporter to learn who Hannah's friends really were, and then who Hannah really was.

Miley didn't want that. She didn't want

that at all. It would be too easy for an unsuspecting Lilly and Oliver to lead people to Hannah Montana's true identity. That would ruin everything.

She turned to Lilly. "Fix him!"

"Why can't you fix him?" Lilly asked.

They heard an announcement from the stage. "Once again, give it up for Hannah Montana!" Her break was over.

"I'm a little busy right now," Miley said. She took the stage again as her fans cheered. She gave a great show, as always. But the entire time she was onstage, she worried about what was going on behind the scenes with Lilly and Oliver.

Chapter Two

After two encores, Miley was ready to call it a night. "Thank you! I love you, too!" she said into the microphone. "Good night, everybody!"

The audience was still chanting Hannah's name when she ran backstage.

"So, where's Count Dorkula?" she asked Lilly.

"Well, thanks to your brilliant friend Lola, Count Dorkula is no-more-kula," Lilly said.

Oliver ran over. He wore a baseball cap, a fake patch of hair on his chin, a big, baggy jacket and low-slung pants. Lots of rings completed his hip-hop look. Just to make sure people believed his disguise, he started to rap.

Miley rolled her eyes. "You couldn't have found a costume that covered his mouth?" she asked. Then she looked closer at Oliver's chin. "What is that beard made of, anyway? Armpit hair?"

Oliver chuckled nervously. "You said nobody could tell," he said to Lilly.

"Well, you're lucky I found this," Lilly said, pointing to his outfit. "Oh, and by the way, I kind of promised your stage manager a raise," she told Miley.

Just then, the stage manager walked by, frowning. He had given up his clothes for Oliver's disguise, and now he was stuck wearing the Dracula costume. Not only was it a ridiculous outfit, it was way too small on him.

"It's all good, Dougie D!" Lilly called.

"This is awesome! Thank you so much," Oliver told Miley. "Watching from backstage was so . . . so . . ."

"Okay, well," Miley said, "Hannah backstage rule number one: be calm. Be cool. Be—"

Lilly let out a high-pitched scream. It wasn't calm, and it wasn't cool.

"Anything but that," Miley finished.

"Look! Look!" Lilly said, grabbing Miley's arm. "It's Guillermo Montoya!"

"*Oooh*, he is so cute!" Miley said.

Guillermo caught her eye from across the room and winked.

Miley grinned back.

Oliver shook his head. "You are such

girls. He's the number one tennis player in the world, and all you care about is how cute he is."

Lilly nodded. Now Oliver was catching on, she thought.

"Yeah, what's your point?" Miley asked.

"Hannah Montana," Guillermo called as he walked over. "Guillermo Montoya," he said, then kissed her hand.

"You don't have to tell me," Miley said, smiling. "I know who you are."

"I know you know. But I like saying it," Guillermo said. "Montana. Montoya. Montana. Montoya. You try it. It's fun."

Lilly and Oliver both tried it. "Montana. Montoya. Montana. Montoya," they chanted together.

"Not you!" Miley said.

"Oh, who are your colorful friends?" Guillermo asked.

"Well, Guillermo, this is Lola Luftnagle," Miley said.

"You can call me Gui," he said, taking Lilly's hand and kissing it.

"Gui—*eep*!" Lilly said with a squeal.

"Very smooth," Miley whispered to her. "And, Gui, this is my friend, um . . ." All of a sudden, she realized she didn't know Oliver's fake name.

Neither did Oliver. When he originally planned his disguise, he was Count Dracula. Now he needed a different name. He looked around for inspiration and saw a microphone stand. "Mic stand," he said with a nervous chuckle. "Mike Stand . . . Lee," he stammered. "Mike Standly, the Third."

"And hopefully the last," Lilly said.

Suddenly, Oliver started to rap, trying to stay in character.

Miley put one arm around Lilly and the other around Oliver. She forced herself to smile. "My friends. Aren't they . . . something?" she said, for lack of a better word.

"Colorful. Strange," Guillermo said with a chuckle. "I love them! And I loved you onstage tonight. You were like me on the tennis court. A tiger." He leaned toward Miley and growled.

"*Eep!*" Lilly squealed again.

Guillermo's phone rang. "Excuse me," he said.

Miley pulled her friends over to the food table. "He thinks I'm a tiger!" she said happily.

"He thinks I'm colorful," Lilly said. "That just leaves strange for you, Mikey," she said to Oliver.

Guillermo was speaking rapid Spanish

into his cell phone. Miley couldn't understand what he was saying, but she could tell something was wrong from the tone of his voice. She was able to make out a few words, including "Kelly Clarkson" and "*disastre.*"

"*Oooh*, disaster," Miley said. "Doesn't sound good. Even with that adorable accent." She ran over to Guillermo as soon as he hung up. "Is everything okay?" she asked.

Guillermo was so upset he had to take a couple of deep breaths before he could answer. "My celebrity partner for this pro-am sprained her thumb," he explained. "Speed texting."

Celebrity partner? Professional-amateur tennis tournament? Suddenly, Miley had a great idea.

"Well, I just happen to know a celebrity

with a wicked serve and a very cute tennis outfit," she said.

"You're kidding," Guillermo said, sounding relieved. "Hannah, if you can play, you're my new partner."

Lilly gasped. This was too exciting!

"Then get ready to rally, 'cause you're looking at the girl that put the tennis in Tennessee," Miley said.

"Fantastic!" Guillermo hit speed dial on his phone and walked away to share the good news with the pro-am organizers.

Miley took Lilly's hands and squealed. She was going to play tennis with the cutest player in the world!

Oliver wasn't nearly as excited for her as Lilly was. "You don't play tennis," he said.

"And I don't skydive either. But, honey, I'd jump out of a plane with that boy any day," Miley said.

Who cared that she didn't play tennis? She would be sharing a court with Guillermo Montoya. What could go wrong?

At the beach the next day, a woman walked up to Rico's Surf Shop. She was wearing a glittery bandana, a long peasant skirt with a scarf wrapped around her waist, and a white embroidered top. She looked like a gypsy fortune-teller.

Rico was behind the counter drinking a smoothie.

"Excuse me," the woman said, "I'm very thirsty, and I've lost my purse."

"Wow, sounds like you have a problem," Rico said. He took a big sip of his smoothie and then smacked his lips. "Ah. That's good."

"Please, I can't pay, but I'll gladly tell your fortune for a water," the woman said, reaching for Rico's hand.

Rico pulled his hand away. "I already have a fortune," he said. "Why? Because I don't give away stuff for free." He laughed at his own joke, but the fortune-teller didn't find it one bit funny.

She narrowed her eyes at him. "You are an evil little boy," she said. "Because your heart is cold, terrible things will happen to you. Until you learn to be nice, you are cursed!" She moved her arms back and forth, as if she was showering a curse over Rico's head.

Rico mockingly imitated her, then watched her walk down the beach. Her silly curse didn't scare him.

"What was that all about?" Jackson asked as he walked up carrying a boogie board.

"Some scam artist tried to work me for a free water. Now I'm cursed." Rico pretended to be scared. *"Ooooh."*

Just then, a girl ran down the beach past them. She wasn't watching where she was going and banged into Jackson's boogie board. The caramel apple she was carrying flew up into the air. It spun and twirled, then landed on Rico's head, sticking to his hair.

"That was a coincidence," Rico said, shrugging it off.

Jackson was trying hard not to laugh when another kid tripped on a seashell. His caramel apple went flying through the air, too, and landed on the other side of Rico's head. Rico looked as if he had caramel-apple ears.

"Wow," Jackson said, laughing. "How about them apples?"

Back at the Stewarts' house, Miley ran down the stairs grunting.

Mr. Stewart looked up from his newspaper. "What in the Sam heck are you doing?" he asked.

"I'm practicing my grunt," Miley explained. "All great tennis players have a signature grunt." She demonstrated by making a face as if she were concentrating hard, swinging her arms to imitate a tennis serve, and grunting again.

"Well, you sound like Uncle Earl doing his annual sit-up." Mr. Stewart grunted, then used his Uncle Earl voice. "Well, that ought to do it for this year."

"Daddy, come on," Miley said. "I can't help it if I'm pumped. I am going to be serving it up with the cutest guy in tennis!" She clapped her hands together and squealed.

"And it's all for charity," Mr. Stewart said.

"Yeah, I was getting to that," Miley said

dismissively. She was glad that the event was for charity, but all she could think about was that Guillermo Montoya would be next to her on the tennis court.

"By the way, the people from the tournament called," Mr. Stewart said. "They can only get you one ticket."

"One ticket?" Miley asked, sitting next to her father on the couch. "Now I've got to choose between Lilly and Oliver. This ought to be fun," she said sarcastically.

"It won't be a problem, honey. Just tell them the truth," Mr. Stewart said, patting her knee. "They're your friends. They'll understand."

Miley nodded, but she wasn't too confident.

Chapter Three

Mr. Stewart was wrong. When Lilly and Oliver came over a couple of hours later, Miley gave them the news. They didn't understand. They both wanted to go to the tennis tournament, and they were willing to fight for it.

"She's taking me!" Lilly yelled at Oliver. She turned to Miley. "Tell him!"

"She's taking me!" Oliver shouted. "Tell her!" he said to Miley.

Miley looked over at her father, who was sitting on the couch. His advice hadn't worked, and now her friends were mad. "Way to go, Dad," she said sarcastically.

"Now, honey, I said they'd understand," Mr. Stewart said. "I didn't say they'd be happy about it."

"I'm going!" Lilly insisted.

"No, I'm going!" Oliver yelled.

They both turned and shouted at the same time. "Miley!"

Miley grunted in frustration.

"Hey, look on the bright side," Mr. Stewart joked. "I think you found your tennis grunt!"

Miley glared at him. Grunt or no grunt, she felt like a piece of rope being pulled in a game of tug-of-war.

Lilly and Oliver weren't the only ones who

were having trouble getting along. Rico had just made himself a sandwich at the snack bar when a little girl walked up. She had a half-eaten chocolate ice-cream cone in one hand, a crumpled napkin in the other, and ice cream all over her face.

"Can I have another napkin, please?" the little girl asked.

"One per cone!" Rico yelled. "You got a problem with that, use your shirt!"

"You're mean!" the little girl shouted.

"'You're mean,'" Rico said, imitating the girl.

Jackson, who had just finished refilling the napkin dispensers, watched Rico and the little girl with a confused expression. What was the big deal about a napkin? he wondered.

After the little girl walked away, Rico started to put mayonnaise on his sandwich.

He lifted the top piece of bread and spotted a giant, brown, hairy thing.

"Caterpillar!" he screamed. He lifted it up to take a closer look. It was gross! "I almost ate that," he said, gagging.

"You know, I accidentally ate a caterpillar once. Week later, burped up a butterfly," Jackson joked.

"This isn't funny," Rico said. He walked out from behind the counter with a thoughtful expression. He was beginning to see a pattern. "Flying caramel apples, caterpillars—"

"That embarrassing oil stain on the back of your pants," Jackson interrupted.

"What?" Rico yelled. He peered over his shoulder and saw a huge, brown stain on the back of his pants. How many people would believe it was oil?

"*Ay, mami!* I've been cursed!" Rico

screamed. He grabbed Jackson's arms and pleaded with him. "Jackson, you've got to help me."

"How? The fortune-teller said that you were cursed until you learned how to be nice. And I think we both know that's never going to happen," Jackson said.

"Oh, yes, it is!" Rico said, looking determined. He grabbed a napkin, forced himself to smile, and skipped over to the little girl. "There you go, sweetie," he said, wiping her face. "All better."

At that moment, another caramel apple flew threw the air. It sailed over Rico's head and stuck to the surfboard behind him.

"Yes! It worked!" Rico said. Then he remembered a mean thing he had done that he needed to fix. "I've got to go tell Grandma where I hid her teeth."

Jackson watched Rico run off. As soon

as he was out of earshot, Jackson started to clap. All the people who had disagreed with Rico over the last few days stepped forward. The fortune-teller, named Madame Escajeda, the kids who had "accidentally" thrown caramel apples, and the girl with the ice-cream cone were all part of Jackson's plan.

"Bravo! Bravo!" Jackson said. "You were all brilliant. And worth every penny." He reached into his pocket, pulled out some money, and paid his actors. He had hired not only Madame Escajeda, but everyone else, too. It had been an elaborate plan to get back at Rico for all the mean tricks he had played on Jackson.

Now, not only had Jackson gotten back at Rico, he had made sure that his boss would give him a few Saturdays off.

A pretty girl jogged by. "Hey, Jackson.

Can't wait for our date on Saturday."

Jackson smiled. "Me too, Steph."

"You did all of this just to get one Saturday off?" Madame Escajeda asked.

"Of course not," Jackson said.

Another pretty girl walked by, a blonde this time. "Hey, Jackson. I'll see you next Saturday," she said.

Jackson smiled at her and then turned to the fortune-teller. "I did it for all the Saturdays," he said.

Madame Escajeda grinned. Now she was starting to understand.

Jackson misread her grin. "So, what are you doing in two weeks?" he said.

"Oh, I don't see me in your future," Madame Escajeda said. She chucked him under the chin and walked away.

Miley had gone to the beach to try to think

of a solution to her tennis tournament problem. The fact that she didn't really know how to play tennis didn't bother her. Having just one ticket and two best friends did. Finally, she decided to flip a coin.

"Heads I take Oliver, tails I take Lilly," she said aloud, flipping a quarter into the air. The quarter landed on a table—on the coin's edge. It wasn't heads or tails. "Oh, come on!" Miley said, looking up.

After leaving the Stewarts' house, Lilly had gone home to think about how she could convince Miley to take her and not Oliver to the tennis match. When she had a plan, she went to the beach to find Miley.

Oliver had done exactly the same thing. He ran into Lilly near Rico's Surf Shop. They both tried to be the first one to reach Miley.

"Stop pushing!" Lilly yelled, shoving Oliver. "Get out of my way!"

"Move out of my way," Oliver told her.

Lilly pushed past him and ran to her friend. "Hey! Hey, Miley, I made you a cake!" She set a plate down on the table. The cake was triple Dutch chocolate, Miley's favorite. "Look, it has hearts on it," Lilly said, pointing to the icing.

"Oh, real subtle," Oliver sneered. "Buttering her up with a cake with hearts. Pathetic!" Then he pulled something out of his pocket. "Here, Miley, I made you a shirt."

The T-shirt was printed with a picture of Oliver and Miley. There was a rainbow over their heads and the words BEST FRIENDS underneath their smiling faces.

"She's taking me!" Lilly yelled.

"She's taking me!" Oliver insisted.

"Keep this up and neither of you are going to the tennis tournament tomorrow!"

Miley shouted. She felt like a tennis ball being volleyed from one side to the other.

Oliver sighed.

Lilly narrowed her eyes at him.

Rico walked up to them. "Are you guys talking about the celebrity pro-am this weekend?" he asked.

Miley was too tired to deal with Rico. If he wasn't insulting her, he was usually trying to trick her. She already had too much on her mind. "Not now, Rico," she said.

"Because I have a ticket I'm not using," he said sweetly.

"I said, not—" Suddenly, Rico's words sank in. "Teeny-weeny meanie, say what?" Miley asked.

"You can have it if you want," Rico said.

"What's the catch?" Miley asked. Rico didn't give anything without wanting something in return.

"No catch. I'm going to be spending the day petting homeless cats," Rico said.

Miley crossed her arms and looked him up and down. Was Rico on the level? she wondered. He seemed to be. Finally, she accepted the ticket. Problem solved. Lilly and Oliver could both go to the tennis match. Miley hoped they wouldn't find anything else to argue about once they got there. The match was supposed to be on the tennis court, not between her two best friends!

Chapter Four

"**L**adies and gentlemen, your guest umpire, TV's favorite talk-show host, Collin Lasseter," said an announcer as the tennis tournament began the next day.

The crowd applauded. Lilly was sitting in the audience, dressed as Lola. Today's wig was bright red. Oliver sat a row behind her in his Mike Standly disguise. Their seats were right off the court, instead of in the stands with everyone else. They were front and center for all the action and on their best behavior. Lilly planned to watch Guillermo. Oliver wanted to see some good tennis.

Mr. Lasseter took the microphone. "Thank you, and welcome to the United People's Relief Celebrity Pro-Am," he said. "Taking the court, Andy Roddick and his partner, the adorable Dakota Fanning."

There was more applause. Oliver looked around for Miley. He knew that she and Guillermo would be playing against Roddick and Fanning.

"And entering from the north side, Guillermo Montoya and his partner, in her first appearance on the pro-am circuit, America's songbird, Hannah Montana!" Mr. Lasseter announced.

Guillermo jogged out onto the court. Miley skipped behind him. Her blond wig had been styled into two long braids. She wore a lavender tennis skirt and a tank top embroidered with an *H* and an *M*.

Oliver jumped to his feet. "All right, Hannah!" he shouted, loud enough to be heard above the rest of the crowd. "Hannah, sitting prett-ay in the cit-ay!" he called. He motioned toward his seat to indicate how great it was.

Lilly rolled her eyes. He was going to totally embarrass their friend. She stood up. "Will you have some class, please?" she yelled.

Miley ran over. "Hey! It sounds like you guys are having a great time," she said. "You want to know how I know?"

Neither Lilly nor Oliver could answer her.

"Because I can hear y'all from all the way over there!" Miley said from between clenched teeth.

"Sorry," Lilly said.

"Got it!" Oliver told her.

Miley didn't understand why they were still fighting. "The main thing is, you guys are my friends, you guys are here, and you have awesome seats."

"You're right," Oliver agreed. "And it's all too—"

At that moment, a tall woman wearing a large orange hat sat down in front of Oliver, completely blocking his view.

"Are you kidding me?" Oliver said.

"Oh, boy," Miley said. Why did she think this was somehow going to turn out to be her fault?

Guillermo ran over. "Hannah," he said. He took her arm and smiled at Lilly. "Excuse us, *senorita*."

Lilly grinned.

Guillermo led Hannah back onto the court. "One little itty-bitty thing," he said.

Then his smile disappeared and he looked very serious. "Guillermo Montoya never loses!" he said. Just to be sure Miley understood, he said it again. "Never!"

"Never?" Miley asked. "Not even a little charity game? You know, for fun?" She tapped his arm with her tennis racket, trying to get Guillermo to laugh. "*Hee, hee.*"

Guillermo didn't laugh. "Fun is for losers," he said seriously. "I'll take care of Roddick. You make Dakota cry more than she did in the pig movie." He looked across the net, smiled, and waved. "Hi, Dakota!"

When he turned back to Miley, he looked intense again. "Aim for her head," he instructed.

Miley objected. This was supposed to be a fun game, not a death match. "I'm not going to aim for her —"

Guillermo was walking to his side of the

court. Suddenly he turned and stared at Miley with a crazy look in his eyes.

Now Miley was scared. "Okay," she said meekly.

The match was just about to start when Oliver tried to get Lilly's attention. He didn't think it was fair that Lilly got to watch everything and all he could see was the back of a stranger's head. "*Psst*!" he whispered. "Switch seats with me."

Lilly turned to him. "Gee, let me think," she said. "No." Why would she give up her seat in the front row to sit behind a lady with a tall hat?

"But it's not fair!" Oliver whined loudly.

"You're lucky you're even here in the first place!" Lilly shouted. "Now stop talking to me!"

Lilly and Oliver suddenly realized

everyone at the match was watching them instead of the tennis court.

"If you two are finished," Collin Lasseter said.

Lilly and Oliver both gave him an embarrassed smile.

"First service, Hannah Montana," Mr. Lasseter continued.

Miley bounced a tennis ball on the ground, then tossed it into the air to serve it. Just as she raised her racket to hit the ball, a phone rang. She missed. The phone was Lilly's.

"Hey, cutie with the tomato head, turn off the cell phone," Mr. Lasseter shouted.

"Sorry! Forgot to put it on vibrate," Lilly said. She flipped the phone open and tried to answer quietly. "Hello?"

It was Oliver. "Switch seats with me," he said into his own cell phone.

"You're pathetic," Lilly told him, flipping her phone closed.

Oliver wasn't about to give up. He hadn't come to a tennis match to look at the back of someone's head. All Lilly cared about was how cute the tennis players were, but he actually wanted to see the match. He threw crackers at Lilly and repeated his request over and over again. "Switch seats with me. Switch seats with me. Switch seats with me. Switch seats with me. Switch seats with me."

Lilly caught the crackers and threw them right back.

Miley was raising her racket for her second serve.

"Knock it off!" Lilly yelled at Oliver.

Miley twitched as she swung her racket. Instead of going over the net, the ball hit Guillermo in the middle of his back.

"Love fifteen," Mr. Lasseter said. "It could be a long day."

Miley didn't know much about tennis. But she knew that love meant zero. They were behind Andy Roddick and Dakota Fanning. Guillermo couldn't be happy, Miley thought.

"We're having some fun now," Guillermo said with a chuckle, jogging over to Miley. He pretended to laugh for the fans, then hissed at her under his breath. "I thought you put the tennis in Tennessee."

"I guess I just kind of left it there," Miley said, laughing nervously.

Guillermo didn't laugh.

"Cute outfit though, right?" Miley asked brightly.

"Not cute enough," Guillermo snapped.

Miley dropped her racket and marched over to Lilly and Oliver. She wasn't the world's best tennis player, but their immature fighting kept breaking her concentration.

"Uh, honey, the court's over here," Mr. Lasseter said.

"Yeah, I know. Just a loose lace. Let me just take care of it over here," Miley said. She hopped over to Lilly and Oliver, trying to make it look as if she was tying her sneaker. "Stop talking!" she said to her friends. "You're making me look bad."

"I wouldn't know," Oliver said. "I can't see."

"Well, boo-hoo," Lilly sneered at him.

Miley shook her head. She had to stop this. She turned to the woman blocking Oliver's view. "Excuse me, ma'am, do you mind taking off your hat?" she asked with a sweet smile. "My friend can't see."

"Of course. I'm sorry." The woman took

off her hat, but underneath it, her hair was in a giant mound on the top of her head. It made no difference at all.

"Oh, sweet niblets!" Miley exclaimed. She shook her head in frustration. This situation wasn't getting any better.

Chapter Five

Meanwhile, Rico had finished petting homeless cats and was headed back to the snack shop. He had learned that he was allergic to cats. His nose was so stuffed up that he was forced to breathe through his mouth. The cat hair all over his clothes wasn't helping.

Jackson was wiping down the counter. "Hey, Rico, nice sweater," he teased.

"It's not a sweater," Rico said. "I was

petting cats all day." He sneezed.

Stephanie walked up, dressed for a date. "Hey, Jackson, you ready to go?"

"Uh, yeah. Just one sec," Jackson told her. He climbed over the counter and turned to Rico. "Listen, boss, I've got to leave a little early, so—"

"Don't give it a second thought," Rico said. "But, before you go, I promised a couple of Wilderness Girls I'd find them a ride. Their mom's car ran out of gas, and they need to deliver their cookies."

"Rico, I'm getting ready to leave," Jackson said, with a nod toward Stephanie.

"*Awww*, I was a Wilderness Girl once," Stephanie said. "Jackson, go ahead. I mean, I'll wait."

"Okay," Jackson said with a shrug. "I mean, two girls, how long can it take?"

At that moment, two Wilderness Girls

wheeled a handcart over to Jackson. It was piled high with cartons of cookies.

"Follow this nice man, kids," Rico said, smiling. "I'll go help your mom unload the rest of the truck."

"The tr-truck?" Jackson stammered. Just how many cookies would he have to deliver? he wondered.

Back at the tennis tournament, Oliver was still trying to see past the woman with the giant hair. He leaned to one side and then the other. No matter what he did, he couldn't get a good view. He was still trying to get Lilly to give up her seat. Lilly was as determined as ever not to give in.

Oliver checked the clock on his phone and then leaned forward to whisper to Lilly. "It's been forty-five minutes. Switch with me!"

"No!" Lilly insisted. "I get the best seat because I'm her best friend."

"You mean her greediest friend!" Oliver said, his voice rising.

"Well, it's better than being her dumbest friend," Lilly retorted.

Oliver's voice rose even higher. "Well, I'd—"

A woman interrupted him. *Shhhh!*

Oliver ignored her. "I'd rather be stupid than greedy," he yelled at Lilly.

"Of course," Lilly yelled back. "'Cause you're stupid!"

Oliver gasped.

Miley looked at them from the tennis court. "Will you two just work it out!" she yelled.

While she was focused on Lilly and Oliver, she took her eye off the ball. It hit her right in the stomach.

She leaned over with a groan. "I'm going to remember that, Dakota."

After what seemed like hours, Jackson finally made his way back to the beach. He ran to Rico's Surf Shop, checking over his shoulder to make sure he wasn't being followed by Wilderness Girls. He was covered with crumbs.

He saw Stephanie leaning on the counter of the snack shop, looking bored.

"Steph, you're still here!" he said.

"Jackson, what's that all over you?" she asked.

"Cookies! I didn't drive fast enough, so the Wilderness Girls threw them at me," he said. "But on the plus side, we won't have to buy candy at the movies." He looked at one shoulder and then the other. "Do you like Butter Clusters or Fat Mints?"

"Oh, wait!" Rico said, jumping over the counter. "I promised that little boy you'd get his kite off that tree."

"What?" Jackson asked, looking behind him.

"Oh, and then you have to help me get a beached whale back into the ocean," Rico said.

"But—"

Rico wasn't done with his list of good deeds. "Oh, and also there's—"

Jackson cut him off. "Wait a minute! I know exactly what's going on." He turned to the little boy who was waiting for his kite. "He hired you, didn't he?"

The little boy shrank back. Jackson's harsh tone of voice was scaring him.

"Didn't he?" Jackson demanded again.

"Jackson, what's wrong with you?" Stephanie asked.

The little boy started to cry and ran over to his mother.

"That's right, cry!" Jackson yelled. He was convinced that Rico had hired the boy and that his tears were just an act. "Cry, you little faker! You little—"

Stephanie had seen enough. There was no way she was going out on a date with a guy who yelled at kids. "Jackson, you're . . . you're so horrible!" she said, then turned and walked away.

"Wait, Steph!" Jackson pleaded. "You don't understand! I hired a fortune-teller to scare Rico into being nice. Somehow he found out and now he's trying to get back at me!"

Stephanie just kept walking.

"Steph!" Jackson yelled again.

She was already gone.

"Oh, Jackson, Jackson, Jackson," Rico said, glaring at him.

"All right, who told you?" Jackson asked.

"Actually, you did," Rico said. "Just now."

"What?" Jackson asked. He was sure that Rico had been trying to trick him, not genuinely doing good deeds.

"Up until then, I didn't have a clue," Rico admitted. "Now, I've got a lot of mean to catch up on. And you know what they say." He gave Jackson a menacing look. "Cruelty, like charity, begins at home."

Jackson cringed. If Rico could drive him crazy when he was trying to be nice, Jackson could only imagine what would happen when Rico was really out to get him.

Jackson wasn't the only one afraid that someone was after him. Miley hadn't been doing well at the tennis match, and Guillermo was supermad. She danced from foot to foot, trying to look as if she could actually hit the ball if she had a chance. The truth was that she stank up the court.

"Well, with this serve, Roddick-Fanning could win the match," Collin Lasseter said over the loudspeaker. "*Aw*, let's face it. My dog and I could win the match."

Guillermo walked over to Miley. He pretended to smile for the crowd around them. Miley was the only one who could hear his words, and they didn't match his expression at all.

"I swear, if you cost me this match, I will go home tonight, dress up like you, and hit myself in the face," he said.

"You have got some serious issues, my friend," Miley said. She didn't get what the big deal was. It was just a game, after all.

Meanwhile, in the stands, Oliver lifted up the woman's long dreadlocks and tried to peer between them to see the court.

"Excuse me," the woman said.

"Sorry, I lost a nickel," Oliver said with a fake chuckle. "Keep it." He tried to pull his hand out of her hair, but it was caught. The big rings he was wearing as Mike Standly had gotten stuck.

"What are you doing in my hair?" the woman demanded.

"Sorry, my hand's stuck," Oliver admitted.

"Well, get it out!" the woman yelled.

"Help me," Oliver said to Lilly.

Lilly stood up, frustrated because Oliver was taking her attention away from the match—again. "Like I said, you're pathetic."

Oliver tried to get his hand free without yanking the woman's hair out. Lilly tried to help him, but she made things worse.

"Oh, great, now I'm stuck," Lilly said. "You and your stupid rings."

On the court, Guillermo and Andy Roddick were volleying the ball back and forth. Then Dakota hit a strong backhand. The ball flew through the air in a high arc.

"It's a lob! I got it!" Guillermo said, running forward.

Miley saw it, too. It seemed an easy ball to hit. Maybe she could get out of this match with at least one good hit. "No, no, no," she said, running toward the ball.

"I got it!" Guillermo insisted.

"I got it!" Miley said, bringing her arm back to swing her racket. Her eye on the ball, she banged into Guillermo and knocked him over.

At the same time, Oliver and Lilly finally managed to get free of the woman's hair. Except it turned out to be a wig, and as they pulled their hands free, it went flying into the air. Miley was just about to hit the ball when the wig landed on her face, completely blocking her view.

Miley swung wildly. Instead of hitting the ball, her racket flew out of her hand and hit Collin Lasseter in the stomach. Miley ran into the net, and it ripped from the poles, wrapping around her. She tripped and fell to the ground, tangled in the net. The audience gasped in horror. The announcer declared Andy Roddick and Dakota Fanning the winners of the match.

Guillermo didn't even say good-bye. He stormed off the court without a word.

Oliver and Lilly ran over to make sure Miley was okay. The stands quickly emptied, and the three friends were alone on the tennis court. Miley was still lying on the ground tangled in the net.

"I'm sorry I was jealous," Lilly said.

"And I'm sorry we made this your problem when it was clearly Lilly's," Oliver added.

Lilly cleared her throat.

"And mine," Oliver admitted. He turned to Lilly. "And next time Hannah has one ticket, you should go."

"No," Lilly said. "You should go."

"I said you," Oliver told her.

"No, you!" Lilly snapped. "You're impossible."

"You're impossible-er!" Oliver retorted.

Miley couldn't believe it. They were fighting again. And they had forgotten about her!

"Hello!" Miley yelled. "Girl wrapped in a net here."

Oliver and Lilly stopped their feud long

enough to notice that when Miley had tumbled into the net, she had managed to get herself trapped in it.

They worked together to unravel her. Finally, Miley was free of the net. She looked at Lilly and Oliver and realized things could be worse. She had two best friends who were fighting to spend time with her. That wasn't such a bad problem to have. Miley's friends were what made her secret double life worth every moment. After all, she had the best of both worlds, and she wouldn't trade either of them.

*Rock out with the band
with this awesome JONAS book!*

KEEPING
IT
REAL

Adapted by Lara Bergen

Based on the series created by Michael Curtis & Roger S. H. Schulman

Based on the episode, "Keeping It Real," Written by Roger S. H. Schulman & Michael Curtis

As members of the band JONAS, Joe, Nick, and Kevin Lucas are international superstars. But when Mrs. Lucas feels that their stardom is going to their heads, she decides it's time for some ground rules. Will the brothers have to permanently trade star-studded events for doing dishes? Trouble continues when the boys try something special for their mom's birthday but accidentally ruin all the home movies from their childhood instead! Can they get things back to picture-perfect?